Pirates to the Rescue

By Christophe Miraucourt

Illustrated by Delphine Vaufrey

W
FRANKLIN WATTS
LONDON•SYDNEY

Meet the Crew

Ricky

Melinda

Fatbeak

Gingerbeard

CHAPTER 1
Storm Ahoy!

Standing on the deck of the *Intrepid*,
Melinda took in a deep breath of sea air.
It was the first time that her pirate dad,
Gingerbeard, had taken her on his ship.
Her brother, Ricky, was also on board and
looked worried by the darkening clouds.

"Storm ahoy! Storm ahoy!" Fatbeak

squawked. Suddenly thunder rumbled and

a streak of lightning flashed above them.

"Lower the sails!" Gingerbeard ordered his crew. Soon waves as high as walls were smashing over the ship.

"I am Melinda the Terrible, daughter of Gingerbeard, granddaughter of Blackbeard and great-granddaughter of Redbeard. I am ready to fight the storm!"

But that wasn't Gingerbeard's plan. "Get inside at once, you sprogs!" he yelled out over the whistling winds.

For hours the *Intrepid* swayed from side to side, creaking loudly. Melinda and Ricky rolled about in their beds.

Finally the sea calmed and they fell asleep.

The ship was very quiet when Melinda
woke up. Ricky was still asleep. When
Melinda peeped through the window, she
was amazed to see a strange-looking island!

"Wakey-wakey, little monkey!" Melinda
called to Ricky.

"Little monkey!" Fatbeak repeated
as Ricky woke up.

CHAPTER 2
Gingerbeard is Missing

Melinda and Ricky saw a mess when they went onto the ship's deck. The mast was broken and the sails were torn.

"Where's my dad," Melinda asked Pegleg, the old pirate who was busy sewing one of the sails back together.

"Where's Dad?" Fatbeak squawked, landing on a cannon.

"He went ashore to find drinking water," said Pegleg.

"Where are we?" Ricky asked.

Pegleg shrugged his shoulders.

"The storm took us here," he said.

"We could be anywhere!"

"I knew having a girl on a boat would be bad luck!" Eyepatch the pirate grumbled.

"When did Dad go?" Melinda demanded.

"He should have been back by now," Pegleg admitted.

Melinda looked at the island. She could see the sandy beach where Gingerbeard had left his boat. Behind, there was a gigantic forest full of trees and a huge mountain towering over everything.

"Dad could be in danger," Melinda said to Ricky. "What if he needs our help?"

"I don't know…" Ricky trembled.

He remembered the crocodiles and snakes

they had come across in their

other adventures.

Melinda spun round to face the crew.

"Pirates!" she cried, "let's go and find our captain!"

"We came here to find treasure," Scarface replied, "not to babysit our captain!"

All the crew laughed at Melinda.

"All right, I'll go on my own," said Melinda bravely. As she climbed down to a rowing boat she paused and turned to Ricky.

"Are you staying here or are you coming with me?"

"I'm coming with you!" Ricky shouted, getting on the boat.

CHAPTER 3
A Strange Island

Melinda and Ricky landed on the island near Gingerbeard's boat.

"Let's follow Dad's footprints," Melinda suggested.

Soon the footprints led them to the edge of the thick forest. Melinda looked back at the *Intrepid* in the distance and stopped. It was tempting to go back to safety. Melinda took a deep breath and said: "I am Melinda the Terrible, daughter of Gingerbeard, granddaughter of Blackbeard and great-granddaughter of Redbeard. I am not scared!"

Ricky looked around and said: "I am Ricky! Son of Gingerbeard, grandson of Blackbeard and great-grandson of Redbeard. And... I'm a little bit scared!"

Suddenly, Melinda stopped. In front of her a few tree branches had been broken and the grass had been trampled on.

"Gingerbeard must have had a fight here," she said. Ricky looked nervous. "These branches were cut with a sword," he added.

"Hurry up!" Melinda cried. "Dad may

be in trouble."

Melinda and Ricky continued into the forest

until the path divided into two.

"Oh no, which way do we go?" Ricky asked.

Melinda wasn't sure but Fatbeak suddenly

squawked above them: "Scarf to port!"

"It's Dad's scarf!"

Ricky cried out.

"He's left us a clue!"

Melinda said. "He

knew we would

look for him."

They took the left path and soon reached
a cliff with a rope bridge leading to the
other side.

"Someone must have built this bridge,"
Melinda thought out loud.

"So there are people on the island!"
Ricky exclaimed. Ricky and Melinda
looked nervously at each other. What if
Gingerbeard had been kidnapped?

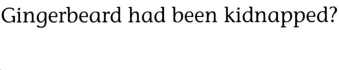

The bridge didn't look very safe. It was made out of wooden planks and ropes. Melinda carefully stepped onto the first plank, which creaked underneath her like breaking bones.

"Just don't look down!" she told Ricky.

"Too late," he mumbled back, white with fear, as he looked across to the other side where Fatbeak had safely landed.

Slowly and carefully, the children crossed the bridge. They could feel it shaking beneath them. When they reached the other side, Fatbeak squawked excitedly: "Gold at starboard!" Melinda looked up to find a golden chain hanging from a tree branch.

"That's Dad's necklace!" Ricky cried out. "He definitely came this way!"

"Let's keep on going!" urged Melinda.

CHAPTER 4
Trapped in the Forest

The forest grew thicker and Melinda and Ricky had to cut their way through with their swords. All of a sudden, a round object the size of a cannon ball landed at their feet, followed by another, and another.

Soon another ball whizzed past Melinda, but this time she was ready: with a swing of her sword, she sliced it in two. It was a coconut!

They heard a tiny shriek from above and looked up. Perched in a tree was a monkey wearing a necklace, and it was laughing at them. It threw another coconut and disappeared into the trees.

Melinda and Ricky
set off again, but were
soon forced to stop by
a rushing river
crossing their path.
Melinda grabbed
a vine and shouted
to Ricky:
"Follow me!"
She swung on the vine
and crossed the water
easily. Ricky clung onto
another vine and
swung safely
over the water.

Moments later, they heard a loud, pounding rhythm:

BOOM BOOM PACK!
BOOM BOOM PACK!

Ricky and Melinda had reached a clearing where a group of men and women were shaking maracas. Children were throwing spears at a target.

"Look!" said Ricky, pointing at the little monkey with the necklace, who was now tapping on a tambourine. "Hide, Ricky! It might see you!" Melinda warned him.

A girl Melinda's age appeared, dressed in colourful clothes. A big, tall man was following her, and all the other villagers bowed to him.

"He must be the leader," Ricky whispered.

The monkey with the necklace jumped onto the chief's shoulder.

"What do you want, Tam-Tam?" the leader asked the monkey. "A banana?"

"Oh no!" Melinda gasped. "Look! Dad is tied to a pole!"

As Ricky moved forward, a twig snapped loudly under his feet. Immediately Tam-Tam let out a loud shriek and pointed to where Melinda and Ricky were hiding.

"They've seen us!"

Melinda cried.

"Run!"

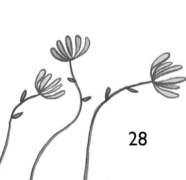

Before Melinda and Ricky could move, spears surrounded them. The young girl with the colourful clothes was threatening them with her weapon.

"Well done, Eloa!" the chief told her.

"I am Eloa, daughter of Whampackwhizz – chief of the Boom-Boom-Pack tribe! Drop your weapons at once!" she exclaimed.

"How can you speak our language?"

Melinda asked, surprised.

"You aren't the first strangers to visit here,"

Eloa responded. "Follow me."

Eloa walked them towards the pole where

Gingerbeard was tied up.

"Kids!" the pirate cried.

"We're so sorry," Ricky
apologised. "We wanted
to help but we failed."

"I hope you are not too
disappointed?" Melinda asked her dad.

"How could I be disappointed?" Gingerbeard said. "You were the only ones to come to my rescue – you are true pirates."

Meanwhile Eloa was tying Ricky and Melinda to another pole.

"What are you going to do with us?" Ricky asked Eloa.

"We're always in need of extra hands to carry the wood or repair the huts. But first of all, we'll throw a big party to celebrate your capture!" she said.

Soon the same loud pounding rhythm filled the air again.

BOOM BOOM PACK!
BOOM BOOM PACK!

As their kidnappers were busy singing and dancing, Melinda tried to untie her ropes. She noticed Ricky wriggling about.

"What are you doing?" she asked him.

"I hid my pocket knife in my boot," he said.

"I'm trying to reach it." At last, Ricky

managed to bend down far enough to grab

his knife. At the very last minute he dropped

it out of reach. "Oh no!" he moaned.

Just then Fatbeak flew
to the rescue. He picked
up the knife and gave
it back to Ricky.

"Thanks, Fatbeak!" Ricky said, and then he cut his ropes, before setting his sister and Gingerbeard free.

"Let's grab our weapons and get out of here while no one is looking," Gingerbeard told his children.

But Tam-Tam, who was eating a banana on the roof of one of the huts, saw them escaping. It told the tribe immediately.

"Our prisoners have escaped!" Eloa bellowed,

seizing her spear.

"Back to the ship, quickly!" shouted Gingerbeard.

CHAPTER 5
The Rescue

The pirates ran as fast as they could, with
Eloa and the tribe close behind them.
They reached the rushing river again.
Gingerbeard grabbed a vine and swung
across, followed by Ricky and Melinda.

Just as they were about to enter the forest again, Melinda heard a scream and a loud splash. Eloa's vine had broken and she had fallen into the water!

Melinda thought quickly. She knew that they had time to get back to the ship safely, but she also knew that Eloa might drown if she didn't help.

"Help!" Eloa cried. Melinda acted fast. She cut down a vine and threw it towards Eloa. "Grab the vine, quickly!" she shouted. Eloa caught hold of the vine and gripped it tightly. Melinda pulled Eloa slowly out of the water.

When Melinda looked round, she realised that Whampackwhizz and his men had surrounded Ricky and Gingerbeard.

"My darling Eloa!" he cried, dropping his spear to squeeze his daughter in his arms.

Then he turned towards Melinda: "You saved my little girl's life! You are as brave as a Boom-Boom-Pack! We must have a party in your honour to thank you."

That night Whampackwhizz's tribe threw a big party. Gingerbeard and his crew brought some rum and Whampackwhizz supplied some tasty and exotic fruits.

Eloa and Melinda invented the *Dance Aboard!* dance, while Ricky played a snakeskin drum. The party went on until morning.

Over the next few days, Whampackwhizz's men taught the pirates to dance,

and Eloa gave Ricky and Melinda some music lessons.

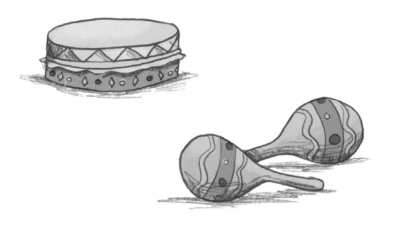

In return, Melinda showed Eloa how to use a sword.

Tam-Tam taught fatbeak how to throw coconuts. They became great friends.

Gingerbeard's present to Whampackwhizz, a pirate flag, was placed on the roof of the chief's hut. Melinda gave Eloa her headscarf as a present.

In return, Eloa gave Melinda a whistle carved from some precious wood.

"So you can think of me every time you blow it!" Eloa explained.

The next day, the *Intrepid* started its journey back home. Melinda suddenly spotted her headscarf on the sandy beach. It was Eloa!

"I am Eloa, daughter of Whampackwhizz – chief of the Boom-Boom-Pack tribe! And I am your friend!" she cried.

Melinda, holding back tears, replied:
"I am Melinda the Terrible, daughter of
Gingerbeard, granddaughter of Blackbeard
and great-granddaughter of Redbeard.

And, one day, I'll come back to see you!"

As Melinda looked back the island was already becoming smaller, but she would never forget her new friends.